SPIRITED AWAY

SPIRITED AWAY:
FAIRY STORIES
OF OLD NEWFOUNDLAND

by TOM DAWE

with illustrations
by VESELINA TOMOVA

To my brother, Charles, and sister, Mary. We grew up together
in the old house where the stories came.

    ~ T. D.

To my brother, Georgi, and the endless summers of our childhood.

    ~ V. T.

CONTENTS

IN A PLACE LIKE THIS

HOW CLEARLY IT COMES BACK TO ME: the abandoned two-storey house at the edge of the meadow, by the brook with its shady pool where Grandfather fished for eels. He often dried the eel skins to make laces for his boots.

As a young girl, I thought eels were snakes, and I'd jump back each time he pulled a big one from the murky water. I shivered when the thrashing creature coiled around his arm, as he removed the hook. Sometimes one would slip from his grip and disappear into the boggy ground. Grandfather looked funny down on all fours, falling on his face now and then, sputtering, trying to drag the escaped eel back by the tail. But fun was scarce for a girl of ten in a place like this.

"It's a place of spirits and evil fairies," an old woman once told me. She was standing on the wooden bridge not far from the derelict house. "They come seeping up from the ground when the mist is rising. I've seen them myself. And you might see them too, conditions being right. No wonder the people moved away. Said they saw lights dancing in the night, down by the water where the fairy pipes grow."

I was a timid, sensitive child; such talk made me all the more fearful. My mind never rested. Each time I gazed across the meadow at the front of the house, the dark, empty windows appeared to be watching me, eyes in a gray, sagging face.

"You're always seeing things," Grandfather used to say.

I watched as small birds flitted in and out through the windows. When afternoon shadows deepened, they roosted on a ledge that ran across the front of the house, a couple of feet above the door. That ledge. There was a story going around about it, and the thought of that story always had me watching for something more than birds. Late one afternoon, it was said, a young fellow, leading his horse home from grazing, saw a small bent figure, no more than a couple of feet in height, walking, wobbling duck-like, on that ledge. It came out of one window and went in through another. The frightened horse stopped dead in its tracks, refusing to budge, no matter what the lad did. Then the animal bucked, rearing back, almost yanking the reins from his hands. The figure had come out through the window again. A small grizzled man, all in green, standing there in eerie silence, looking down on them.

Tugging frantically on the reins, the young fellow took no time for a closer look. He turned away, grabbing off his cap to cover the horse's eyes. It was the only way, people said, that he could get the horse to move past the accursed spot.

There were other stories,
stranger still. People spoke of a wedding
in the house years ago. No musician
had been available to play for the dance,
and they were trying, in the old way,
to make do with chin music. Later
in the night, however, a strange man
carrying a tin whistle walked into the
room and started to play. Immediately
the chin music ceased, and up-tempo
dancing began. All through the night,
the stranger played his music. Jigs and
reels and every kind of tune. Everybody
was out on the floor. Such dancing as
they'd never done before. As the jigs and
reels went on, people became exhausted,
falling all over the place. But they kept
on dancing; nobody could stop. They
danced and they danced, until the sun
came up. Then, in a flash, the stranger
was gone. "The Devil," some said later.
But others called him "the Fairy Man."

The old tales were playing on my mind during our last visit to the place. We came to make the hay that morning. Father had an agreement with the owner to cut one last crop. He and Grandfather were busy spreading the hay, taking it out of pooks or haycocks, for another day's drying in the sun. Mother, who was raking up a few strands around the edge of the meadow, told me to watch my baby sister, Hazel, asleep on a blanket in a clover patch. I settled back in the warm grass near the blanket and gazed around me. The day was filled with a sweet scent of hay and wild roses.

I was dozing lightly when, abruptly, I came out of my slumber to see a greenish butterfly hovering above the blanket. I sat up and watched it. It was beautiful. I leaned over for a closer look, and it rose into the air, fluttering off towards the brook. I got up and began to follow.

But I was stopped in my tracks, moments later, by the baby's crying. I turned and ran back. Hazel was screaming and kicking her legs. I didn't know what to do. She grew worse and worse, her screaming more frantic. Suddenly Mother rushed by me and picked her up. It was then we saw it—her arm, hanging like the broken wing of a little bird.

We were in a panic. Nobody knew what happened. What a terrible time we had that day. Seems like it took forever to get back home. The paths were long and winding; the dirt roads rough.

Later in the evening, the doctor was impatient when none of us could tell him what had happened to Hazel. She was still crying even though he had given her something for the pain. "Like a blow with a stick," he said, examining her and carefully setting her arm back in place.

Long after the doctor had gone, I crept out of bed and put my ear to the floor, listening. The voices down in the kitchen were low and serious.

"I'll never go back to that place again," Mother declared. "We're lucky she's still here, poor Hazel. I hope she's too little to remember any of this. I wish I could say the same for the rest of us."

I shivered there, alone in the dark bedroom, pressing my ear even closer to the floorboards, unable to make out what Father was saying.

"We'll haul out the hay tomorrow. Then we'll be done with it," Grandfather said.

After all the years, the gray abandoned house, the meadow, and the winding brook are etched in my memory. Sometimes they seem static, still, like a painting. And then, a solitary old man moves out of the alder bushes, shuffling towards a weedy pool.

I close my eyes to look again. I smile to myself. I know that man. And I know that he's got a crumpled page from a Bible and a coiled eel-line somewhere deep in his pocket.

MUSIC MAN

IN OUR COMMUNITY, PADDY, THE HERMIT, was a local legend. He lived just outside our cove, in a mossy cabin in a droke of woods. We called him the music man, a spry, wiry fellow who'd mastered a number of instruments, above all the tin whistle and harmonica. My father used to say that Paddy could make the mouth organ talk. Mother called him a wizard, and he was sure to turn up whenever there was a time or a dance.

On occasion, if he found himself in a situation where no instrument was available, Paddy would make music out of anything. One winter in the lumber woods, he entertained the bunkhouse crowd with music he made from combs, saws, bottles, and spoons, whatever came to hand.

When I was a child, lying in bed at night, how comforting it was to hear the familiar strains of Paddy's harmonica in the distance, coming around the cove, as he made his way home in the dark. I'd be waiting there in the ticking gloom, wide awake, with all kinds of frightening thoughts going through my mind. I'd worm down under the heavy quilts, covering my head to avoid shifting shapes across the wallpaper, and creaking sounds in the shingles and rafters. It seemed

like I was the only one awake in a wide, mysterious world. And then I'd hear Paddy's spirited music going by, dispelling all my fears.

But there were times also, when he visited our homes and seemed to enjoy scaring us. When he was in the mood, nobody told scarier stories than Paddy. One night he played at a kitchen party in our house. It was a Friday night, so my brother and I were allowed to stay up late. When the party was over and he was leaving, he turned around on the doorstep.

"Do you know what I'd like tonight?" he asked. "I'd like to see a spirit or a fairy or something. I'd walk up and put my hand right through it."

Afterwards, Father laughed and said, "Paddy had a bit too much to drink. He's bad enough when he's sober, getting on with his old foolishness." My brother and I were horrified. We just couldn't see anybody being that devil-may-care, even Paddy. Imagine, he was going out into a night as dark as the grave, not one bit afraid, or so he said, of anything living or dead. He was even looking forward to a ghostly encounter!

Eventually, we found out that he'd been repeating the same wild fancy in other night kitchens. But we didn't know that Paddy's wish would soon be granted.

It was a mid-summer night, not a trace of moon or star in the sky. Paddy was strolling home late from a concert in the parish hall, blowing away on his harmonica. He was crossing the meadow in front of his cabin when, suddenly, he found himself in a crowd, a bunch of youngsters, he thought at first, up to their games. Figures emerged from the shadows. A host of little people formed into a ring around him. In the gloom it was difficult to see them but he soon knew who they were. Paddy's careless bravado had beckoned the fairies.

Now they were dancing to his music. He was the hub of a wheel; they were the rim. And, strangest of all, he couldn't stop playing: jig after jig, reel after reel, one flowing into the other. He was held there in a spell as the minutes flew by. He started to sweat. His energy waned. Swaying in the mesmerizing frenzy, he felt himself sinking to the ground, dropping his harmonica, grabbing at a tree branch as he fell.

From where he lay on the grass, he gazed up at them, a host fading away.

And then, he saw one of them turning back, as if taking a last sideways look at him, a figure taller than the others, hunched, bent over to blend in with the circle. This face was the last thing Paddy saw, a fleeting, marble glow in the moonless night, somebody from an old photograph, somebody long dead, now dancing with the fairies. Somebody he ought to know. Somebody he...

And then, in an instant, it all melted away.

When Paddy woke up, bewildered, shivering in the gray dawn, the robins were chattering about him. He picked up his harmonica and wiped it on his sleeve. He had slept all night in the settling dew, on a grassy mound not far from his doorstep.

Over the years, Paddy told his story many times. People, especially the older ones, said he was never quite the same after that harrowing night. Others said his music changed. Father and a few of his cynical friends were unconvinced. To them, once again, Paddy simply had one drink too many.

But we children were terrified by the story. We still listened to the old believers, they who were never dismissive, they who were never afraid to entertain the shadow.

THE MARSH

MY FIRST TEACHING POSITION was in a small, one-room school on Birchy Island. I was seventeen that fall, and homesick most of September, even though I boarded with a kind, elderly couple in Western Bight, Mr. and Mrs. Blake.

Originally the island had two communities, Western Bight and the now-abandoned Eastern Brook, still connected by a mile-long trail, snaking across a marsh in the centre of the island. Throughout the fall I often hiked down to Eastern Brook, sketchbook in my pocket. I grew to love the area, trekking there in all weathers, particularly on Saturdays when I could relax. These were green times, heady days, fraught with many pleasures. The landscape was pristine, beautiful in silver ocean light. A few derelict buildings remained, like the small church with its steeple bell intact. I explored old walls, foundations, and headstones. Later in the season, I would fish for sea trout in the river and the nearby pond. I loved having the place all to myself. Eventually, however, I came to learn that I wasn't entirely alone there.

One rainy November night, just before bedtime, the Blakes and I were having a cup of tea, and Mr. Blake was telling me about the marsh.

"It divides the island into two parts," he said, "running from woods to sea. I think that, only for the marsh, the livyers of Eastern Brook wouldn't have moved away like they did. Everyone says the marsh is haunted, my son."

This took me by surprise. What, I wondered, was coming next?

"According to an old story," he continued, "in the days before settlement, a gang of pirates killed a man there. They tried to push the body into a cask and sink it in the marsh. But the barrel was too small, so they cut off the man's head to make it fit. Then they stuffed head, body, and all into the barrel and sank it. Years after, it was said that a headless man used to rise out of the bog on misty nights, wandering the trail between our place and Eastern Brook."

"But I have to say," Mrs. Blake chimed in, "nobody from this place ever saw the headless man. Our stories are mostly about the fairies. They've been in the marsh a lot longer than the poor pirate. I think the fairies took his spirit with them. They do take over the dead sometimes, you know."

"People hear sounds like drumming coming off the marsh at night and on dark, foggy days, too," Mr. Blake added. "Some joke

about it, saying the fairies are tapping on the old pirate's drum. But it's no joking matter. At times the taps are slow; other times they step up, like a wild dance."

I gathered a number of strange stories that winter. Soon I was writing them into my journal, along with sketches, bird sightings, and nature-studies. Since Birchy Island was open to the North Atlantic, winter was always stormy, the ideal season for yarns by the fire, stories of the little people carried on the blast, laughing, singing, making weird music. In fact, any noise you heard outside, while you were snug in bed on a stormy night, could be the fairies.

According to the islanders, Jack-o'-Lantern, or "Jacky," was one of the most frightening fairies of all. The eerie lights that hovered above the bog could lure you to your doom. And could have other dire consequences, as well. On dark nights they were often seen floating around the stones in the graveyard: "corpse candles," omens of death. Mr. Blake said the lights appeared in Eastern Brook churchyard the night before several of the community's fishermen were lost at sea. People saw the lanterns through their windows, floating eastward from the marsh.

"That year there were only four or five families left in Eastern Brook," Mr. Blake said. "They all moved away soon after. Some of them left in such a hurry they even left their crops in the ground. They went to the States and never came back."

An elderly woman in Western Bight used to recount bits of fairy lore she heard long ago in childhood. It chilled me when she wondered aloud: "Who or what owned the hand gripping the lantern?" There was a dreadful demon on the other side of the light, she claimed; it was better not to get too close.

21

I'll always remember the last story Mr. Blake told me. It was a spring evening and we were walking home together from a trouting trip down in Eastern Brook. The sea trout were plentiful and I wanted to stay a bit longer. But he was determined to get home before dark. It was coming on duckish when we passed the marsh. A light drizzle was falling, and night birds were calling through the fog. I noticed how much more relaxed he became as we approached Western Bight.

"Back when I was a boy," he said, "two young fellows from Eastern Brook were going home late one night, from a dance in our school, when they got the fright of their lives." He paused.

"What happened?" I asked.

"A strange light, just above the ground, followed them, from the marsh all the way home," he answered. "They escaped by taking refuge in the church. Back then, the church door was never locked. So the boys were lucky. No fairy would dare come inside the Lord's house. Yes, my son, they had to stay in the church all night. Can you imagine those boys there in that big dark building, with whatever light there was playing on the stained glass above the altar? And each time they dared to look through the window, they could see that light hovering above the graves, winding in and out among the headstones. Whatever it was, it never left until the rooster crowed the next morning."

It seems so long ago now, that wondrous evening on Eastern Brook, fishing for sea trout with Mr. Blake, listening to him spinning yarns about Jack-o'-Lantern.

"Why do you call him 'Jacky'?" I asked.

He looked at me and smiled. "We have to give him a name, the same as we do when we call the devil 'Old Nick.' Because, when we give him a familiar name like that, it takes away some of our fear. He's an awfully dark spirit, my son."

A FAIRY FUNERAL

WHEN WE WERE CHILDREN, everything scared us. The harmless dragonfly, for example, was called "the devil's darning needle." The creature hovered all around us in the summertime, ready to sew up the ears and lips of disobedient children. To us, even a common snipe, owl, or bittern calling from the marsh, might be a voice from the other side. We counted crows for the stories their numbers told—"one for sorrow, two for joy" and seven was "the story yet untold." Death omens were everywhere: we were uneasy when a dog howled at the moon, a bird flew into a room, or the night wind cried like a banshee outside our clapboards. And how we dreaded dark, rainy nights when knotty chains of frogs went helter-skelter across the road, hopping on ancient webbed feet on their way to a fairy spree.

We always made sure we got home before dark, especially when we had to pass the place where a narrow path to the graveyard branched off from the main road.

We'd heard about what happened to a woman at this very spot one evening just before dark. As she walked along her solitary way, her spirits were suddenly lifted when she saw people coming up the road towards her. Just in time, she thought, as she quickened her pace to join them. Now she'd have company when she passed the graveyard lane. But, something stopped her dead in her tracks. The people were moving, phantom-like, in a slow march, off to her left. In shock, she realized she was watching the rear end of a funeral turning in towards the graveyard. She stood there, mystified. This was too late in the day for a funeral. Besides, she hadn't heard of any recent death in the community. This can't be, she thought. But all she could do was watch.

The frightened woman couldn't see a coffin or any people at the front of the procession. They had already moved up the narrow path through the dark trees. But those at the back, and now closest to her, looked to be the size of small children, a hushed column of mourners. Stranger still, as they passed by, they seemed to be fading, shadows moving across shadows. Not one of them looked in her direction. And she didn't recognize any of them.

This, she realized, was no ordinary funeral. Everything raced through her mind. Could it be a fairy funeral, she wondered. It was unlucky for mortals to see any kind of fairy activity, and many times she had heard it said that such an apparition was a dreadful omen, a sign of death for the one who witnessed it.

The woman turned around to go back, but she couldn't move. Her pounding heart rose up in her throat. She could hardly get her breath. She watched, terrified, as the last of the strange procession disappeared up the path.

Struggling back that evening, she kept staring straight ahead, afraid of what might be around her. It was as if frog, snipe, and cricket, the breezy birch and juniper, were calling her name. But finally, somehow, she made it home.

This incident happened years ago in the small place where my friends and I grew up. It was never made clear to us if the woman died soon after her encounter with the fairies. Some people vowed

that she did. Through the years, however, we heard other versions of the story. One old man used to say that fairy coffins were usually open, and if the woman was the one about to die, she would have seen herself laid out in the box. So perhaps it was lucky, he said, that she met the back of the procession instead of the front. But he was in the minority. Many others believed that seeing the corpse didn't matter; just the sighting of a fairy funeral was one of the darkest omens of all.

As I said, we children, who believed in "the devil's darning needle," made sure we were always among the obedient ones, safe at home long before the spirits and fairies came out. And our elders, whose stories were a mixture of entertainment and warning, never let us forget it.

BONES

I **WAS A WAR BRIDE** when I came to Newfoundland with my husband in 1946. We were young and optimistic, looking forward to a life together in the small outport where he grew up. But I was not prepared for the weather. It was foggy most of the time, and storms pounded in from the open Atlantic. Day and night, I could hear the undertow hissing, just outside our flimsy walls, and great waves spilling on the rocks.

During the first two or three weeks, I complained most of the time. I couldn't help it; I fell into depression. Perhaps my demons had followed me across the water. Eventually, I took matters into my own hands. I worked hard to get to know more people in the community, and settled in. The sun even peeped out, occasionally.

One wet, windy night in late September, after my husband had gone to bed, I was alone in the kitchen, spinning, when a knock came on the door. It startled me. Who in the world, I wondered, would be out on a night like this. I stiffened, standing there, with my hand on the spinning wheel, waiting. Rain slapped the window pane.

A minute or so passed, then the knocking started again.

"Who's there?" I called, stepping timidly towards the door.

"Do you have any bones?" the voice, an old woman's, asked.

I was speechless, growing more alarmed by the second, imagining what the old woman outside the door might look like—there in the dark, with rain running down her face.

"I want bones," she called out hoarsely. "Bones for a pot of soup, missus."

I still couldn't speak. Hurrying across the kitchen, I blew out the lamp and ran upstairs. All out of breath, I roused my husband from his sleep, fiercely panting that an old woman was banging on the door.

He jumped up and sat on the edge of the bed, confused, groggy, not quite getting what I was saying.

"An old woman's down there, demanding bones," I cried. "She's whining like the banshee."

"Oh, that's just Abigail," he replied, a look of relief on his face as he slid back into bed.

"Abigail? Who's Abigail?"

"A poor old woman who lives by herself, out by the lighthouse," he said. "She's lived there as long as I can remember. She goes house to house, sometimes, looking for a bite to eat. She has no sense of time. She must think this is November, 'blood month,' when we slaughter the animals for the winter. Most people are good to her, though some call her a witch just because she lives by herself, away from the rest of us. Young boys have even thrown rocks at her house."

"Why would she come here so late?" I asked.

"That's the way she is. People say she's out all night, roaming with the fairies. Abigail was normal, the same as you and me, when she was a little girl, they say, until one fine day, when she was out in the yard playing while her father chopped wood. Suddenly, a sound came from the top of the hill, a hollow galloping sound. Abigail called out to her father that she was going to go up to see the horses. She ran up the hill, but there were no horses to be seen.

"Her father tried to stop her, but it was too late. A strong gust of wind came out of nowhere, catching her up, spinning her around in a whirl of leaves, sticks, and dead grass. After that, she was never the same."

Long after the old woman had gone, my husband and I lay there in bed, sleepless, not saying a word. I never knew there was such a multitude of sounds in a clock's ticking.

Next morning, he asked me why I had been so upset last night.

"I couldn't help it," I replied. "The old woman brought back a darkness from my childhood."

"What do you mean?" he asked.

"Back in the West Country, we children were always told about an ugly creature, 'Bloody Bones'—the most evil fairy of all, a skinless, long-tooth goblin who lived in a dark cupboard under the stairs. He crouched there, blood dripping down his face, sitting on a smelly pile of bones, the bones of naughty children who used bad words or told lies. We were warned he would grab us if we even peeped at him through the keyhole."

My husband smiled. "It's one thing to have fairies in the woods and marshes, or riding by on the wind. It's quite another thing to have one living in the house."

"Yes, there I was, out in the dark porch, not sure if the door was locked, trembling by the keyhole. And a strange, old voice on the other side of that door, crying out for bones."

FALLEN ANGELS

WHEN WE WERE TEENAGERS, and not much interested in the yarns spun by our elders, we laughed at Uncle Andrew's stories. Uncle Andrew had a unique take on everything. I remember one Christmas Eve night in particular. A couple of friends and I were in the kitchen playing cards when he came in, asking if we knew what was going to happen out in the stable when the clock struck midnight. Of course we'd all grown up with that Christmas legend.

"This is the night when angels sing and animals speak," he said, settling into the most comfortable chair by the fire. "I bet none of you fellows is brave enough to go out there tonight," he chortled.

"Would you?" I asked him, while my friends grinned. In our smug way, we knew what was coming next.

"My son, I wouldn't venture out there tonight for the world." He paused to tap ashes from his pipe. "I know you lads make light of it all, but let me tell you something. I heard of a scoffer who hid away in a manger one Christmas Eve to find out for himself. Well, sir, he got such a fright he never wanted to talk about it again. Overnight, his hair got as white as the driven snow. Is there anything more shocking,

I wonder, than hearing animals speak, especially when you yourself are in the conversation."

We kept playing our cards, smiling to ourselves, half-listening as he prattled on. We'd heard it all before, beastly predictions for the year ahead and further. And on it went. We stuck to our cards and games of divination, but Uncle Andrew, for pious reasons, had no time for these.

"Tonight the animals will be like the fairies," he said, "not to be fooled with."

"But surely, Uncle Andrew, you don't expect the fairies to pray tonight?" He had some weird ideas concerning the fairies, but this was the first time I'd heard them included in Christmas.

Uncle Andrew paused, folding his arms before he replied. "No, my son, I just meant the animals would have fairy powers on this special night. Of course, fairy animals roam around all through the year. I've heard of fairy cats and dogs, and birds too. They say a great white stag once followed a woodsman around all one day. Later the man said it was a fairy creature, a good luck sign, indeed. People used to say that the fairies were fallen angels, cast out of heaven for siding with Satan. You see, fairies are half-way beings, stuck here on earth, between heaven and hell. On a clear night you might see them linked in a chain, arms and legs hanging down from the horn of a quarter moon. Some are kinder than others, and they like it when we call them the 'Good People.'"

Uncle Andrew was upset by the cynical looks on our faces. He glowered at us a moment or so, but then carried on with his stories.

"A fellow was walking home by himself one night. It was in the dog days and the air was mauzy. By and by, he heard voices coming from some raspberry bushes by the side of the road. When he peeped in through the tangle, what a surprise he got. He saw a ring of little people, some dancing and others boiling a kettle. A cluster of unfriendly faces looked up at him, and he jumped back. But, as he did, something struck him on the temple. One of the fairies had thrown the kettle at him. My son, he got out of there as fast as he could. When he got home and looked in the mirror, he had a sooty cut on his forehead, about the size of a fifty-cent piece. Over the weeks, it faded a bit, but, God bless the mark, it stayed on him for the rest of his life."

Uncle Andrew droned on, yarn after yarn, throughout that night long ago. I regret now that we didn't pay more attention. But my friends and I were seriously into our card game, nodding absently as he talked.

However, later in the night, we did perk up somewhat. By then he'd gotten into a story about a poor young man out in the woods cutting sticks on Christmas Eve, when a great shadow passed over his head. Looking up, he saw a big raven perched in a black spruce, shaking snow down on him.

Uncle Andrew paused to refill and light his pipe.

I was watching a wisp of snow drift under the porch door when the clock chimed midnight. A silence came over the kitchen. Wood cracked in the stove, and frost wove a feathery pattern on the windowpane. It was Christmas Day.

Uncle Andrew got back to his story: "The young fellow was surprised by the size of the raven, its feathers shining in the winter boughs. He threw a snowball at the creature, but missed. The bird never moved. So, the fellow went back to his pile of sticks. He was chopping away, chopping away, when a raspy voice spoke down from the tree. When he looked up, the raven was still there, its eyes glowing red. Getting pretty uneasy now, the lad turned away, but couldn't get back to his work. Next thing, he heard the voice again. When he looked this time, he saw a strange little man, just the size of a child, sitting on the limb where the raven had been. 'Do you know who you are?' asked the little man, brushing snow from his cap. 'You are the seventh son of a seventh son. Do you know what that means?' The young man said nothing. He didn't know what the stranger was talking about. 'You shouldn't be living in poverty,' the little man said. 'You have special powers, my boy. You can be anything you want. You have the power to cure evil and all kinds of disease. You can predict the future. Sure, you can even find gold with the flick of a hazel switch... I'll tell you what, if you listen to me, we could work together. We'd have people coming from everywhere, begging for our help. All you have to do is let me guide you. What do you say?' But the lad remained speechless.

He knew that the thing perched in the tree was evil. So he turned, in a wink, and ran out of the woods."

After the way my friends and I slighted him so many Christmas Eves ago, it might seem odd that I should be telling Uncle Andrew's stories today. But, wherever he is now, I know he's forgiven us.

A few nights ago I had a crazy dream. I was in the winter woods and Uncle Andrew was up in a tree, grinning from the shadows as he shook snow down on me. He never said a word.

"Look at himself up there, hiding away in the boughs," I said, laughing. "Who's the old fairy man now?"

Big flakes of snow started to fall, and thicken. The wind freshened, shaking the limbs. And, in no time at all, everything became lost in the whiteness.

SPIRITED AWAY

I'M JUST BACK FROM MY SON'S HOUSE on the other side of the cove. They've been doing some celebrating over there today, I must say. What a time! After six girls, they finally got a boy. I always believed that seven was a special number. Now here I am, a woman in my sixties, with my first grandson. He's worth waiting for; must be close to ten pounds.

Just to be on the safe side, I brought over a Newfoundland five-cent piece, my first gift to him. I put it on a small chain; "to wear around his neck," I said, "as a good luck charm." I wouldn't dare mention that this was to keep the fairies away. If I talked like that, they'd laugh at me, especially my daughter-in-law. She doubts the fairies exist, even more than the others do. But me? I believe the fairies are still around us, in the woods, the marshes, and even our gardens. I had an uncle who said you could never get a good look at them, they'd stay in the corner of your eye, like a glint of light on a leaf or a tremble of a twig. Of course the modern world scoffs at such stuff. But my grandchildren, bless their hearts, still ask me questions, especially about the time their great great grandmother, my own grandmother, was taken by the fairies. I must have told them the story dozens of times, but still they keep asking.

Poor Gran, little did she realize what was in store for her that day we went berry-picking years ago. It was a fine morning in early

September, not a breath of wind on the water. Father was up at daylight, to tackle the horse and get everything ready. In those days, berry-picking was no picnic, I can tell you that. We children had to sell berries to buy boots for the winter. Though it was hard work, it was the best of times for me. I enjoyed every minute, because we stayed out of school until the picking was over. And Gran, young in spirit, looked forward to those times, too. How pleased she was, sitting with us in the middle of the cart, beaming as she adjusted her straw hat. In no time, the horse was trotting along, carrying us off the main road, bumping through rocky places, rattling along green paths and low-bush barrens. We could almost smell the blueberries, big bunches bending the bushes, there for the picking. Gran used to call them "herts," and we laughed at that.

By lunch time we had most of our buckets filled. Even my young brother, Sam, not a very good picker, filled his emper twice. Father lit a small fire and boiled the kettle while Mother spread out a tablecloth for our meal.

After lunch, my two sisters and I decided to go to the top of a ridge where we'd seen big patches of berries earlier. Mother, Father, and Sam had already gone in over the hill. Gran said she was tired, and if we didn't mind, she'd stay a spell by the fire and take a nap.

"I'll see you by and by," she said, in a tired voice. "Go on now with your sisters. Perhaps I'll have another cup of tea."

So we went our separate ways, never thinking that when we all got back later in the afternoon she'd be gone. The fire dead. And Gran nowhere to be found. The whole family fanned out through the woods, calling her. Father kept reminding us that she knew the area too well to go astray, but I'll never forget his worried look. We searched and searched, but we knew as the light waned we'd have to give up.

Finally, with evening settling in, we had to leave without her. I was tormented by the thought of Gran there by herself in the dark. It was almost too much to think about.

On the ride back, the slow pace of the horse tortured me. Even the chirping of the cart wheels seemed to be mocking me, chanting over and over, something sad and terribly lonely.

But what a surprise when we got back home. There was Gran, large as life, out in the yard! She couldn't have walked all that distance on her own, I thought. Yet there she was.

Right away I saw that there was something different about her. She was leaning on the kitchen-garden fence, staring off into the distance. She didn't even look towards us. I was frightened that it might be her fetch we were seeing. But it was Gran all right.

She seemed confused when we all questioned her at the same time. There was no doubt Gran had a story to tell, but we'd have to wait for it. In fact, she'd tell it in bits and pieces, over the remaining few years of her life. So I'll go back to that day and piece it together for you.

Gran said she was taking a nap on a patch of turf when she was awakened by a sound like tapping on a drum. She sat up and looked around. She listened closer. The only sounds were flies buzzing and bees murmuring in the dry grass. A breeze went by, swirling ashes around the cold kettle. Then she saw something that upset her:

Her bucket was overturned. The berries she'd worked so hard to pick that morning were scattered all over the ground. She stamped around the empty bucket. Who would do such a thing, she wondered. Suddenly, a strange feeling came over her.

She found herself walking slowly away from the spot. On and on she drifted, deeper into the woods, as if a wind was at her back, pushing her along. And she was powerless to do anything about it. She was on an invisible path, gliding through tangle after tangle. Not once did she feel a branch or twig even brush her face.

Poor Gran had no idea how far she travelled. She told me one time she thought we were there with her, because she heard voices all around. Later, she'd recall snatches of singing, and music too, the sweetest she'd ever heard.

When she finally came out of the woods, she saw a meadow and a boy of fourteen or so, fencing a small garden. She didn't know the boy, but she soon recognized the place. She was in the next cove, three miles or more to the east of our own community.

The boy was surprised to see her limping towards him. "I was in berry-picking, my son, and I went astray," she said. "I'm from up the shore."

"Looks like you've come a long way, ma'am," he replied, laying down his mallet.

"I must have gone astray," she repeated. "Imagine that...how did I get away down here?" Gran was coming to her senses now, surveying the landscape around her.

"How did you cross the rivers?" he asked. "There're two deep rivers between this cove and yours. They come out through the country for miles. You would have had to cross them both."

But Gran remembered no water at all. "I must have taken another path."

The boy was puzzled. "There's only one trail between our communities and it follows the coast pretty well, ma'am. In fact, there's no path where you just came from. A woman your age wouldn't make it through that tangle."

She stood there, dumbstruck, while the boy hurried off to get his father.

When he arrived, the boy's father also found it hard to believe what she was saying. But he was a kind, understanding man. He brought her over to the house for a cup of tea and a rest, while he tackled up the horse and cart to take her home. And so that's why she was there, waiting for us, when we came out of the woods that evening.

For days, all around the two communities, everyone was talking about Gran's strange journey, how she was "fairy-led." She wasn't the same after that fateful day, they said, and she never picked another berry for the rest of her life.

   As the years passed, her name came up whenever talk turned
to the fairies. Many the raw night, when wood roared in the stove
and wind whistled down the chimney, people wondered about my
grandmother and the time she was spirited away.

THE CHANGELING

YEARS AGO, I CAME TO FAR-OFF NEWFOUNDLAND as a nurse from the British Isles. From my nursing station, I travelled, in season, by boat and dog team, covering a wild rugged coastline of bays and inlets, visiting many small fishing communities where medical services, aside from those offered by local charmers, were almost non-existent. But I was young, energetic, and devoted to my calling, and I got along well with the salt-of-the-earth people who complained little of their lot in life. How could I have anticipated what awaited me one cold autumn night?

I recall it all so vividly. I'd been staying over for a couple of days, tending to my patients in Granite Cove. It was early November, my least favourite time of the year, a season my ancestors referred to as "the windy month," a time of short days and all too many long nights when icy rain pelted the shingles and the stove smoked. When I was growing up back in England I had no time for the gloomy piety of All Souls' Eve. And the slaughter of the animals around Martinmas always made me sad. No Bonfire Night or Guy Fawkes celebration could dispel my mood. A stormy November in Newfoundland brought many dismal images back to me.

I was sleeping soundly upstairs in my boarding house when
a loud knocking rattled the front door. A young man's urgent voice,
quavering on the wind, was crying, frantically calling out to me.
It was John Cassidy.

"Sarah, Sarah, you've got to come quick," he shouted.
"Something's wrong with the baby!"

Mrs. Green, my boarding mistress, unbolted the door.
A gust of wind creaked in the rafters. John was all out of breath
and shaking terribly.

"Something's come over her," he kept insisting. I grabbed
my coat and medical bag, and followed him.

Out in the windy darkness, it seemed like an eternity getting
over to the other side of the cove where they lived. So much went
through my mind about little Gracie. She'd be about seven or eight
weeks old now. I remembered the morning she was born, when I laid
her in the crook of her mother's arm. Now, here I was, praying over
and over that she would be alright, as I held on to John's jacket and
stumbled through the dark.

We finally arrived at the old Cassidy house. So depressing
it was when I entered the porch. It was freezing, a fishy, briny
dampness clung to everything. In the kitchen, Sally stood sobbing
by the cold stove. She never even glanced at us as we came in.

"Where's the baby?" I asked.

"I don't know, but she's not in there anymore," Sally whimpered,
pointing at the bedroom.

"What do you mean, Sally? She's in her crib, isn't she?"
I insisted, fearing what might come next.

"There's something in the crib...but it's not Gracie," she sobbed.

"What?" I gasped, not believing my ears.

"That's not our baby in that crib," she persisted.

I was dumbfounded. "What are you saying?"

"I think the fairies took her."

For a moment, I was speechless.

"Go in and see for yourself, Sarah." This was poor John speaking now. He pointed toward the bedroom.

I thought I'd heard it all before back home in Britain, stories of humans taken away by the fairies, the little folk who peopled the darkness. But I was not prepared for this...

John and Sally backed away as I took a lamp and stepped into the bedroom. The smell struck me first, a scent of ancient bogs, dead leaves, and mossy rampikes dripping in the rain. It was as if the doors and windows were all open to the elements, but as far as I knew, all windows and doors were shut. A chill went to my bones.

The crib was covered by a white, lacy curtain. I couldn't see the baby from where I stood. Fear rooted me to the spot. I stood there in the middle of the floor for a minute or so. I could hear voices and the footsteps of other people from the community coming up the back steps. And Sally still sobbing out in the kitchen. Poor John, in his own grief and confusion, was trying to calm her down.

Finally, I found the courage to approach the crib. I pulled back the sheet. And then, God protect us all! I'll never forget the sight.

It was Gracie all right. She was lifeless, no doubt about it, but she was also changed. The more I looked, or tried to look, the less she seemed like the baby I'd known. An awful foreboding came over me.

I moved quickly around the crib. Dear God, I couldn't describe it! In the flickering shadows the form seemed twisted. The face looked

46

old. Perhaps my eyes were playing tricks on me, but it struck me that a small wrinkled woman was in the place where the baby should have been. I jumped back and hurried out of the room, closing the door behind me.

Out in the kitchen, I had to take control, so I sent one of the young men to get the minister. A pall hung over everything. A few people stood around whispering to each other. Some of them tried to comfort the couple. Soon Sally was escorted over to her mother's house. John followed later. Nobody went into the bedroom until the minister came. The rest of us remained and made plans for sunrise.

Next morning, a small wooden coffin was prepared for the baby. It was sealed quickly and lowered into the earth without a wake or anything. Just a brief Christian ceremony conducted by the minister and a few church elders.

Soon the story spread all around the cove. Everyone was talking about the stolen baby. In a few weeks John and Sally moved away to live in a larger community down the coast. Since nobody would live in it anymore, their old house was eventually torn down and the timber burned.

Over the years, different versions of the story spread. Some people said that the old fairy woman in the crib spoke a few dark words and cackled before she passed away. Others spoke of another unusual happening that night. When John opened the back door for his customary look outside before bedtime, a sudden swirl of wind entered the house, causing a picture of the Last Supper to crash to the floor. Still others liked to talk about a bog just across the road from the old house and to point out the exact place where the fairies took the baby.

People who were considered wise in the ways of fairies saw the story as an unusual case. They claimed that fairies often left an identical child in place of the stolen one, a child that, though it appeared normal enough, would grow up to be unduly cross and troublesome. I can speak only for myself.

I know what I saw. And I know what happened. John and Sally lost their only child. And that night in an outport years ago, I witnessed an evil transformation. Something ugly and strange was left in the cot where Gracie was supposed to be.

SOLOMON USED TO SAY that it was hard sometimes to tell the difference between the fairies and spirits of the dead. They were all on the same track, he said. Once he told us of a cove, an abandoned community on a foggy coast, where ghosts of the people who had once lived there still roamed the lanes and roads, and woe to anyone who pitched a tent there on a spirit path.

Solomon liked to tell about his first experience with a fairy path, when he and his brother were youngsters on a trouting trip. When evening fell, they were comfortable in their canvas tent on a meadow above the river. Later in the night, however, strange noises started, sharp lashes on the sides of the tent, one after the other, like whispering crowds going by, striking out as they went. The boys huddled in their blankets, too terrified to look outside. On and off, all night long, the noises continued, but they clung to each other, until the first sign of daylight. These were the fairies for sure, he said, lashing out with their gaddy whips, angry that someone had camped on their path.

As a young boy, before I went to school, I was scared of Solomon. He was a raw-boned, solitary trapper who knew the deep woods behind our community. Sometimes, anticipating a warm cup of tea and a chat with my father, he'd appear at our house with a bleeding partridge in a brin bag, or a stiff brace of rabbits slung over his shoulder. And I'd run as fast as I could to my mother to get away from him.

The pungent aroma of wood-smoke and turpentine remains with me still, blending in with a whiff of frankum. His damp, greasy coat shines in the doorway. And Mother is telling him once again to leave his big furry cap out in the porch.

But Solomon, like an old mariner back from an unforgettable voyage, needed to tell his stories. Snug in my mother's arms, I listened, becoming braver as the night wore on, listening in the yellow lamplight as he conjured things back from the dark spruce, things that could give a child nightmares.

Some evenings, he seemed preoccupied, even ignoring us, as he described a small cabin in a clearing far back in beaver country, "where water ran the other way."

"I was following a rabbit's path late in the day when everything changed," he said. "All of a sudden the trail widened out into what looked like a common woods path that hadn't been used in a long time. Yet, there were troubling signs of something else. When I bent down to get a closer look, I could see that the bushes and turf were flattened down, but not by human feet, my son... I knew what that path was. It was shining before my eyes. I'd better get out of there, I thought, but I was too far in the country to go home that day. So I said I'd pack up my gear and head out early next morning. I didn't mind leaving the cabin, it was just an old tilt anyway. Still, it was prime country. Had hunting and fishing like nowhere else. A wonderful spot. Water like the springs of Eden before the serpent came."

I was too young to understand everything Solomon talked about, but the fairy path gave me chills. I can still hear him describing his last night in the tilt.

"I never slept a wink that night. Right away queer things began to happen. A couple of times I sat on the edge of the bunk with my feet on the floor. I was never frightened in the woods before, until now. Everything went through my mind. I thought of the man who got lost years ago not far from there. He was never found. And his grandson disappeared in the same place years after that. I heard a trapper say one time that you could hear lost souls in the cry of the loon. It's hard to describe, my son, but something was calling me. Something coming from a long ways off. Even the ringing in the little brook sounded strange to me now. Like music I'd never heard before. Familiar things became unfamiliar. Don't think me foolish for what I'm saying, but all of a sudden, I got the urge to run through the door. That's how queer it was. But, thank God, I held myself back and prayed for morning. If I'd gone through the door that night, God only knows where I'd ended up. I was like Jacob in the Bible wrestling all night with some outlandish power. I wouldn't even look through the window until morning broke and the birds were singing...And then I took off for home as fast as I could."

All this was a long time ago. Solomon is gone now, as are the fairies themselves, who have faded from the modern world and its technology. I think of him when I'm alone in the country and a loon yodels across misty waters, or an owl questions from a distance. I see the juniper tops all pointing east. He used to say that a man wouldn't get lost in the woods if he took his bearings from those trees. But even juniper was no charm against the fairies.

Just yesterday, in calm October sunshine, I was surprised by a small, sudden gust of wind. It whirled from the edge of a clearing, spinning sticks, dead leaves, and grass, disappearing across a meadow.

"A fairy squall," Solomon would say, "the fairies are dancing."

GLOSSARY

ALL SOULS' EVE: November 1ˢᵗ, the day before All Souls' Day when the medieval church remembered souls in purgatory. November 1ˢᵗ is also called All Saints' Day, the day after Hallowe'en, when ghosts and goblins are abroad in the night.

BANSHEE: a female spirit or fairy in Gaelic folklore; her wailing outside a house was an omen of death in that family

BONFIRE NIGHT: the night of November 5ᵗʰ, known as Guy Fawkes Night, on which people light large bonfires. It is an old custom from Britain, celebrating the discovery of the Gunpowder Plot, a failed attempt to blow up king and parliament in 1605.

BRACE: a pair

BRIN BAG: a burlap sack made from course fibres of jute, flax, or hemp

CHANGELING: a child exchanged for another by the fairies

CHARM: something worn for its magical effect of repelling evil or the fairies

CHARMERS:	people with the ability to cure ailments by "charms" or other supernatural means
CHIN MUSIC:	humming or singing of nonsensical syllables by one person to provide lively music for a dance when no instruments were available
DOG DAYS:	warm, sultry period between mid-July and mid-August when the Dog Star (Sirius) rose and set with the sun
DROKE:	a wooded valley or dense grove of trees; sometimes called a "drook"
DUCKISH:	dusk or twilight
EMPER:	a small container, emptied often into a larger container while berry-picking
FAIRY-LED:	dazed, confused, lost in familiar territory; led astray by the fairies
FAIRY MAN:	a changeling, often a fellow with great musical skills, especially on the tin whistle
FAIRY PATH:	a clear woodspath, though little used by humans
FAIRY PIPES:	immature ferns; fiddleheads
FAIRY SQUALL:	sudden gust of wind on a calm day; a small whirlwind or "fairy dance"
FETCH:	an apparition or ghost of somebody, usually seen before or soon after that person dies
FRANKUM:	the hard resin of a spruce tree, sometimes chewed as gum
GADDY WHIP:	a whip made from a gad, a slender, swishy stick

GAMES OF DIVINATION:	games, frequently card games, predicting the future; these were often played at Hallowe'en or through Christmas, or at times that marked turns in the year
GOD BLESS THE MARK:	a phrase said while making a potentially hurtful remark about someone's physical defect
HERTS:	blueberries—also called harts, hirts, horts, or whorts
HOST:	a crowd, group, or multitude
LIVYERS:	inhabitants, dwellers, or permanent settlers of the Newfoundland and Labrador coast
MARTINMAS:	November 11th, St. Martin's Day— associated with wine and food, and the time of year when animals were slaughtered and preserved for the long winter
MAUZY:	damp and warm; foggy and muggy
OMEN:	a sign, token, or forewarning
OUTPORT:	a Newfoundland settlement out in the bay, other than the chief port of St. John's
PAGE FROM BIBLE:	a Christian (or holy) protection against the fairies
POOKS:	small haystacks
RAMPIKES:	standing dead trees
SPELL:	a short rest; break from work or other activity
TIME:	a communal celebration or merry making, sometimes referred to as "a spree"

UNDERTOW: the seaward pull of retreating waves breaking on the shore

YARNS: tales or stories

YOUNGSTERS: originally a term for "green men" or "boys" sent out in the early British migratory fishery to Newfoundland, it now refers generally to children or young people

NOTES ON THE STORIES

IN A PLACE LIKE THIS

This story is set on a piece of property that once belonged to our family in Conception Bay. My mother, as a little girl, used to watch her grandfather catch eels in the dark pool winding through the marsh where rushes and fairy pipes grew. On that land was an "unlucky," abandoned house where nobody could live peacefully. It was said that, over the years, a number of people "died before their time" in that house, and according to ancient belief, their angry spirits hung around, haunting the spot. In this place, a host of fairies was the same as a host of the dead, so evil and malicious that their antics included physical attacks on humans.

MUSIC MAN

The man who told this story about Paddy was a hermit himself, who years ago, in my grandfather's generation, lived outside a small community in the woods of Conception Bay. For him, it was shocking to tempt fate as Paddy did, to boast in the face of dark forces. It made him shiver to think how Paddy's music communicated with the spirit world, even calling up the dead. Unlike Paddy, this hermit was careful to pay due respect to the fairies who sometimes took natural forms such as trees or clouds. He was watchful, for example, when small isolated fog banks floated down the woodspath behind his hut: "I always get out of their way and let them pass," he said. "Once I was cutting wood with a man who wouldn't listen. He walked right into the fairy fog and got smacked in the face. He was never the same after that. People said he had a stroke, but I know the difference."

THE MARSH

In folklore, the nebulous world of swamps and marshes has often been seen as the abode of hostile fairies. In the marshlands of Britain, for example, in Fen Country, the fairies are more malevolent than the fairies in central England who are smaller, gentler creatures. In the marshy fens, the fairies—like "Jack-o'-Lantern"; known also as "Will-o-the-Wisp," "Spunkie," and "Pinket"—are considered dangerous. They hover in dark, boggy places, ready to lead humans astray or to their doom. Years ago, scientists tried to explain these lights away, claiming the flames were nothing more than self-igniting gasses rising from decaying plants, but many people refused to accept this scientific view. One of those people was an elderly woman on an island in Notre Dame Bay where some people in her community were followed by the flickering "Jacky," often in the dead of winter when the marsh was locked under layers of ice and snow. One frosty night she and her friends were forced to seek refuge in a church when the ghostly lantern followed them.

A FAIRY FUNERAL

The woman in this story, like my great grandmother in "Spirited Away," had a reputation for telling the truth. It was a bad omen to meet a phantom funeral; usually it foretold a death, but not always. The woman believed she had met a fairy funeral because those in the grim procession appeared to be small children. Yet, others claimed, using the example of Butler's Marsh on Bell Island, that fairies could also appear in the form of adult humans. Some of the older people believed that only a "special" person, a visionary, mystic, or the like, could see a real fairy funeral. Perhaps like the one the English poet, William Blake, saw in his garden — a procession of tiny, singing people, green and gray, the size of grasshoppers, carrying a body laid out on a leaf, which they buried, before they disappeared.

BONES

The war bride who lived across the road from our house told some horrific fairy stories. Aside from chilling changeling stories, we drew a bit of comfort from the thought that the fairies were far away from us in the woods and marshes. But her stories let them into our homes, hideous beings, lying in the woollies under our beds, lurking in dusty backrooms and dark cupboards under the stairs. The terrible "Bloody Bones" got into my head, ruining many a night's sleep. The war bride had more names for the fairies of her childhood than we had for ours. There were, for instance, the violent "Redcaps" who dyed their caps with the blood of their victims. She even told of vampire fairies and "water kelpies," who took the form of horses carrying their rider victims into fatal waters. Another name for "Bloody Bones" was "Rawhead," included in a traditional nursery rhyme remembered from her childhood:

> *Rawhead and Bloody Bones*
> *Steals naughty children from their homes,*
> *Takes them to his dirty den,*
> *And they are never seen again.*

FALLEN ANGELS

The character, Uncle Andrew, is based on my mother's uncle, an opinionated fellow who had little time for children. We jokingly referred to him as "the fairy man." He sermonized a lot, especially on supernatural issues, and he tended to be melodramatic. As teenagers, my friends and I thought his stories and opinions were silly, but as we got older, some of his darker tales stuck with us, like the one about the raven. After this tale, we were never comfortable in the woods again. To be fair, however, on the subject of fairies as fallen angels, we discovered that Uncle Andrew had a few "experts" on his side. He echoed, for example, St. Augustine's view that the heathen gods (fairies) were not just characters portrayed in idols, but fallen angels trying to usurp God's power. Also, there was an old Irish belief, more harmless, that the fallen angels, though fooled by Satan, were not wholly on his side. Kicked out of heaven, they were not wicked enough for the pit of hell.

SPIRITED AWAY

This story is based on the strange experience of my great grandmother in the woods of Conception Bay South many summers ago. My mother, a little girl who was berry-picking with her, never forgot that day; she told the story countless times throughout her life. Many people in the community believed her because great grandmother was not given to fictions or flights of fancy, and besides, she was known as a person who always told the truth. And nobody could explain how a woman of her age had, unwittingly, crossed a full-flowing river that afternoon. As children, before we grew to appreciate the mystery, we were a little disappointed with the story. We wanted more action, more scary details. We wondered what the fairies looked like. But our elders said that, mostly, the little people stayed in the darkness, or in the corner of the eye; they were tricksters who altered the landscape, meddling in our affairs, like upsetting our pails and buckets, bringing bad dreams, tramping down the hayfields, and tying knots in the horses' manes.

THE CHANGELING

Stealing human babies is one of the cruel deeds of the fairies. This, according to widespread folk-belief, is a matter of survival: fairies have to inter-breed with humans to strengthen their stock. They like infants who are fair-haired, healthy, and rosy-cheeked. In place of the human child, they leave a fairy one, or often, a small, wrinkled old man or woman in the cradle. Sometimes they leave just a rough piece of wood, carved out to look like a child. To the shocked human parents, this weird doll might, for a few seconds, appear to be alive. In addition, fairies will, on occasion, steal nursing mothers to nourish weak, sickly fairy babies. Fairies sometimes lure away skilful young men, and beautiful young girls suitable as fairy brides. From time to time, a male fairy child will be reared into adulthood by a human couple. This person, usually troubled, never fits into the community, though he is often musically gifted, especially on the tin-whistle. He is sometimes called the "fairy man."

WHERE WATER RAN THE OTHER WAY

In the early days of the Newfoundland railway, a few woodsmen and trappers from Conception Bay South took the western train every week to Holyrood. From there, some of them travelled alone across Witless Bay Line, to the Black Woods and beyond, to tend trap lines in "where water flowed the other way." A couple of them perished there under mysterious circumstances. We children were always fascinated by the stories these men and their relatives told. In one case, for example, a wife had a premonition that her husband would not be coming home again. She was alone, knitting him a pair of socks, when a voice whispered to her that he wouldn't be needing socks anymore. She threw the knitting aside and walked over to the window. A few minutes later, she heard a gunshot in the garden near the house, but nobody was out there. More than a week later, searchers found his body in the Black Woods. He had slipped on the rocks of an old riverbed, discharging his gun. Solomon, an old believer in fairies, is based on such trappers and their solitary ventures.

The typeface is Bauer Bodoni;
a revival of the typeface cut by Giambattista Bodoni in 1798,
it was designed by Heinrich Jost for the Bauer Foundry in 1926.
The titling is Veneer.

Designed by Veselina Tomova of Vis-à-Vis Graphics,
St. John's, Newfoundland and Labrador.
Printed in Canada by Friesens.

978-1-927917-13-8

Running the Goat
Books & Broadsides Inc.
54 Cove Road
Tors Cove, Newfoundland & Labrador
A0A 4A0

www.runningthegoat.com